For Kaj Fredrik and his fairy godmothers
—D.L.

For my mom, who knitted baby pink socks when I was inside her

—H.N.

Tell Me My Story, Mama
Text copyright © 2004 by Deb Lund
Illustrations copyright © 2004 by Hiroe Nakata
Manufactured in China. All rights reserved.
www.harperchildrens.com

Library of Congress Cataloging-in-Publication Data
Lund, Deb.
  Tell me my story, Mama / by Deb Lund ; pictures by Hiroe Nakata.
      p.   cm.
  Summary: As they look forward to the arrival of a new baby, a mother tells her young daughter of the
time when they waited for her to be born.
  ISBN 0-06-028876-0 — ISBN 0-06-028877-9 (lib. bdg.)
  [1. Babies—Fiction. 2. Parent and child—Fiction. 3. Pregnancy—Fiction. 4. Birth—Fiction.] I. Nakata,
Hiroe, ill. II. Title.

PZ7.L978718 Wai 2004
[E]—dc21
                                                                                              2002068492

Typography by Al Cetta
1 2 3 4 5 6 7 8 9 10
❖
First Edition

Deb Lund · pictures by Hiroe Nakata

Tell Me My Story, Mama

HARPERCOLLINSPUBLISHERS

"Tell me the story about when I
was inside you, Mama."

"When you were inside me, my belly button popped out because you were such a big baby. People touched my belly like it was a good-luck charm."

"And Daddy touched your belly, too?"

"Daddy put his face by my belly so
he could talk and sing to you."

"Tell about my foot."

"When you were inside me, you were so big and strong that we could see the shape of your foot when you kicked."

"And you were really big, too."

"I bumped into people because I forgot how large I was. And Daddy pushed me up hills when we went for walks."

"How did you get so big?"

"I got bigger because you were growing inside me. I ate lots of food that was white—like crackers, mashed potatoes, rice, and vanilla ice cream—because other food made me feel sick. My belly stuck out so far, Daddy had to lean over to give me hugs."

"Could you see me, Mama?"

"When you were inside me, the doctor took pictures of you with a special camera, and Daddy and I saw you sucking your thumb."

"And we went swimming."

"You swam inside me, and I swam in a swimming pool. Daddy took a picture of me in a bathing suit to send to Grandma."

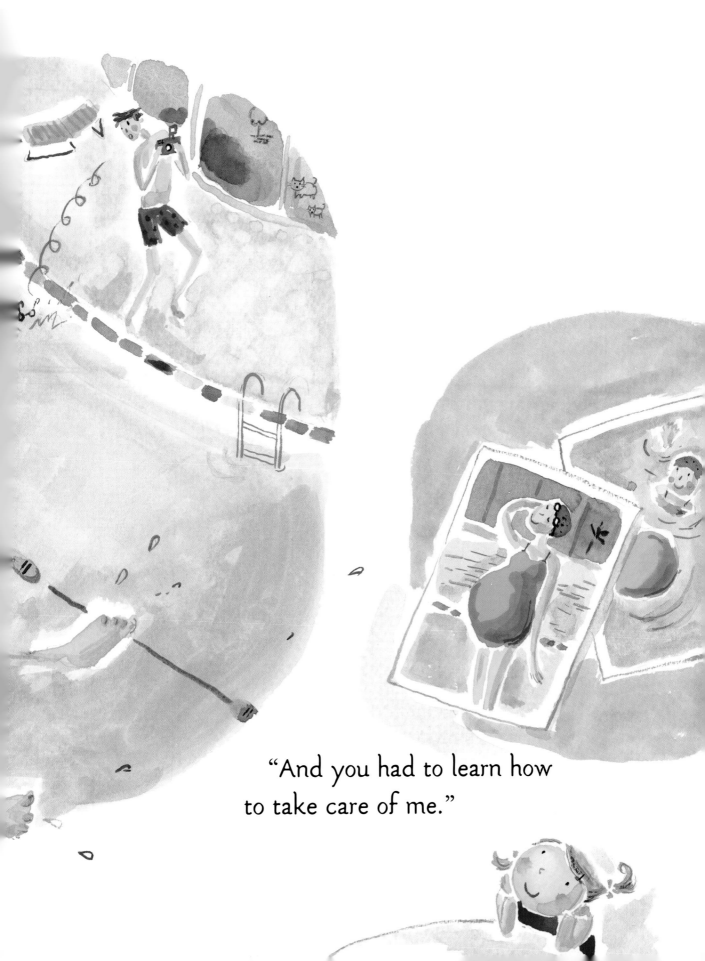

"And you had to learn how
to take care of me."

"When you were inside me, Daddy and I read baby books and went to classes where we learned about being daddies and mommies. Daddy put headphones on my belly, so you could listen to music. Daddy and I picked out names for you."

"And then there was a snowstorm."

"And that's when you were ready to be born. We hiked down our steep driveway in two feet of snow to our neighbors' truck because there was too much snow to drive our own car! Daddy thought you'd have to be born in a snowbank, but we finally made it to the hospital."

"Now comes the special part."

"When we got to the hospital, you were
still inside me. The doctor helped you find
your way out, and it took a very long time."

"And I was mad!"

"You were so mad! When you came out, you screamed at all the doctors and kicked at them with your strong legs. They weighed you and washed you and wrapped you up well."

"And Daddy was there."

"Daddy was there the whole time."

"Now tell me about
the best part."

"The best part was when I saw you for the first time. When you heard my voice, you stopped crying. You took two of my fingers in your fist, and you looked me in the eyes. And when Daddy talked, you looked up at him, too. We all looked at each other, and then we knew what we had all been waiting for."

"Just like we're waiting for the new
baby now, right, Mama?"
"Yes, but the new baby will have its
own story."
"And I'll have mine."
"You'll still have yours."